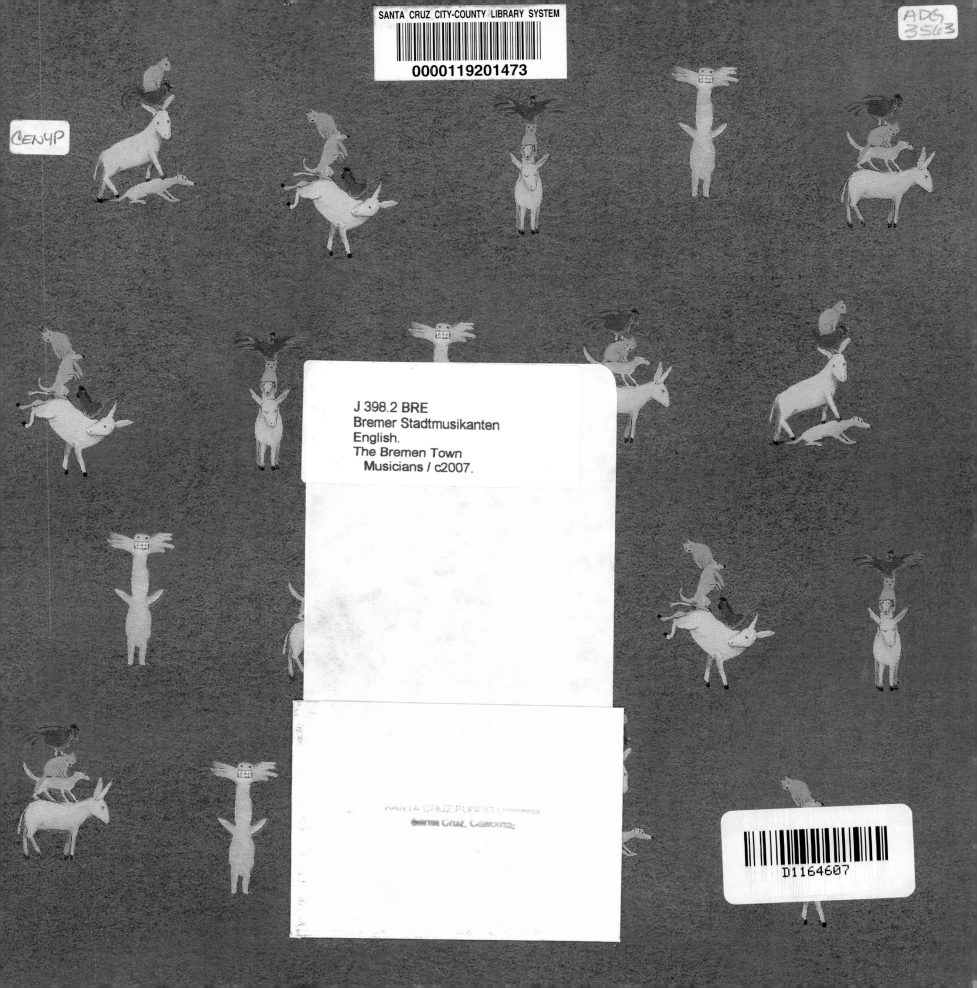

a minedition book

published by Penguin Young Readers Group

First published in German under the title DIE BREMER STADTMUSIKANTEN

Illustration copyright © 2007 by Lisbeth Zwerger

Coproduction with Michael Neugebauer Publishing Ltd., Hong Kong

Rights arranged with "minedition" Rights and Licensing AG, Zurich, Switzerland

Published simultaneously in Canada · Manufactured in Hong Kong by Wide World Ltd.

Typesetting in Silentium Pro by Jovica Veljovic

Color separation by Fotoriproduzione Beverari, Verona, Italy

Library of Congress Cataloging-in-Publication Data available upon request.

ISBN 978-0-698-40042-9

10 9 8 7 6 5 4 3 2 1

First Impression

For more information please visit our website: www.minedition.com

The Brothers Grimm

THE BREMEN TOWN MUSICIANS

Illustrated by

Lisbeth Zwerger

Translated by

Anthea Bell

minedition

Once upon a time a man owned a donkey who had carried sacks to the mill patiently for many long years. However, the donkey's strength was failing now, and he could do less and less work, so his master was thinking of getting rid of him.

Guessing what was in the air, the donkey ran away and set out for Bremen, where he thought he could join the town band as a musician.

When he had been trotting along for a while he met a dog lying in the road, breathing heavily as if he had been running and was quite worn out. "Why are you panting like that, Grabber?" asked the donkey.

"Oh," said the dog, "it's because I'm old, and getting weaker every day. I'm no use for hunting now, and my master was going to kill me. I ran away, but how am I going to earn my living?"

"I'll tell you what," said the donkey, "I'm off to Bremen to be a town musician. Why don't you come with me and join the band too? I'll play the lute, and you can beat the drums."

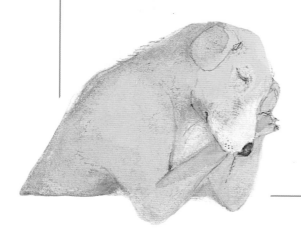

The dog thought that sounded like a good idea, so they went along together.

It wasn't long before they saw a cat sitting by the roadside, looking as miserable as three days of rainy weather. "So what's the matter with you, old Whiskers?" asked the donkey.

"When people are after your life it's no laughing matter," said the cat. "I'm growing old, my teeth aren't as sharp as they were, and I'd rather sit by the stove and purr than hunt mice, so my mistress tried to drown me. I ran away, but now I don't know what to do. Where am I to go?"

"Join us and come to Bremen," said the donkey. "You're used to singing serenades, so you can be a town musician when we get there."

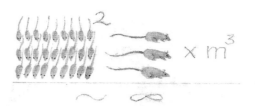

$\times m^3$

The cat liked that idea, and he went along with them. On the road the three runaways passed a farm where a rooster was sitting on the gate, crowing for all he was worth.

"Your crowing is fit to wake the dead," said the donkey. "Why is that?"

"I was foretelling good weather," said the rooster, "but tomorrow is Sunday, and because some guests are coming to dinner the farmer's cruel wife has told the cook to make chicken broth of me. I'm to have my head cut off this evening, and I'm crowing my heart out while I still can."

"I tell you what, Redcrest," said the donkey, "why not come with us instead? We're on our way to Bremen, and you're bound to find something better than death there. You have a fine voice, and if we all make music together we're sure to get by."

But the town of Bremen was too far off for them to reach it in a day, and when they came to a forest that evening they decided to spend the night there. The donkey and the dog settled down under a large tree, the cat and the rooster climbed up into the branches, and the rooster flew to the very top of the tree, the safest place for him. Before going to sleep he looked all around him again, and he thought he saw a tiny spark in the distance. He called down to tell his friends that there must be a house not far off, because he could see a light shining.

"Then let's go and find that house," said the donkey. "It's not very comfortable out here." And the dog thought that if he could find a couple of bones with a little meat left on them it would do him good. So they set off for the place where the rooster had seen the spark, and soon the light was shining more clearly. It grew brighter and brighter until they came to a robbers' house, all lit up inside. The donkey, who was the largest of them, went up to the house and peered through the window.

"What do you see, Greycoat?" asked the rooster.

"Oh, my word!" said the donkey. "I see a table laid with delicious things to eat and drink, and robbers sitting there feasting and making merry."

"We could do with some of that feast ourselves," said the rooster.

"Hee-haw, oh yes, how I wish we were in there!" said the donkey.

Then the animals tried to think of a way to chase the robbers out of the house, and in the end they thought of a plan. The donkey propped his front legs on the windowsill, the dog jumped on the donkey's back, the cat climbed up on the dog, and finally the rooster flew up in the air and perched on the cat's head. When they were ready, a signal was given and everyone began making music:

The donkey brayed, the dog barked, the cat meowed, and the rooster crowed. Then they jumped into the room through the window, and the glass broke as it crashed to the floor. The robbers leaped up when they heard that terrible loud noise, thinking it was a ghost coming in, and they ran away into the forest, scared out of their wits.

So the four friends sat down at the table, helped themselves to all that was left of the feast, and ate as if they might go hungry for the next four weeks.

When the four musicians had finished they put out the light and went to find places to sleep, each looking for somewhere comfortable that suited him. The donkey lay down on the trash heap, the dog lay behind the door, the cat settled on the stove among the warm ashes, and the rooster perched on the top rafter of the roof. As they were very tired after their long journey, they soon fell asleep.

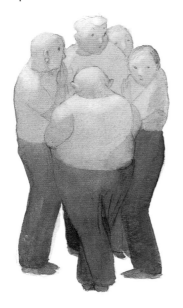

After midnight, when the robbers out in the forest saw that there was no light in the house any more, and all seemed quiet, the robber captain said, "We were fools to run away in such a fright." So he told one of his men to go back and search the house. The man he had sent found nothing stirring, and went into the kitchen for a light. He thought that the cat's fiery eyes, glowing in the dark, were live coals, and he held a match to them to set them burning. But the cat didn't care for that and leaped at his face, spitting and scratching. Terrified, the robber tried to escape through the back door, but the dog lying there jumped up and bit his leg. As he was crossing the yard and running past the trash heap, the donkey gave him a powerful kick with his back leg,

and as for the rooster, roused by all this noise and wide awake, he called down from the rafter, "Cock-a-doodle-do!"

The robber ran back to his captain as fast as he could go, shouting, "There's a horrible witch in the house who hissed at me and scratched my face with her long fingernails. And a man with a knife at the door stabbed me in the leg, and a big black monster lying in the yard hit me with a wooden cudgel, and up on the roof sits the judge shouting, 'Bring the villain into court!' So I ran for it and made my getaway."

After that the robbers dared not go back to their house.

As for the four Bremen town musicians, they liked it so much that they never left again.
And the last man to tell this tale isn't dead yet.